ISBN 1 85854 370 3
Published by Brimax Books Ltd, Newmarket, England CB8 7AU.
Printed in Spain.

FAIRY TALES

ILLUSTRATED BY Gavin Rowe
RETOLD BY Linda Jennings

BRIMAX • NEWMARKET • ENGLAND

INTRODUCTION

Most children love fairy stories. They have grown up with them, and familiar tales such as "The Sleeping Beauty" and "Cinderella" continue to weave their magic well into a child's maturing years. Why are fairy tales so popular? Perhaps it is because they transport the reader or listener from the everyday world into lands of magic and enchantment, where anything can happen – a princess falls asleep for a hundred years, or a hideous monster is transformed into a prince. They are good stories in their own right, with a beginning, a middle, and an end. They have a strong sense of morality – the bad and the lazy are punished, and the good and the industrious receive their reward – an important factor for children, who have an inbuilt sense of justice.

Fairy tales are told the world over, and echoes of the most familiar stories can be found in many cultures. The Brothers Grimm, Hans Christian Andersen and Charles Perrault are probably the best known of the European storytellers, and you will find retellings of some of their tales in this collection.

CONTENTS

	Page
The Sleeping Beauty	8
Hansel and Gretel	18
Rapunzel	27
Rumpelstiltskin	36
Cinderella	44
The Snow Queen	57
Aladdin	71
The Little Match Girl	80
The Ugly Duckling	84

THE SLEEPING BEAUTY

THERE was great rejoicing in the royal palace. The Queen's baby daughter had just been born, and she had been named Rose.

"We must have a big celebration for her christening," said the King. "Everyone in the Kingdom will receive three golden coins in celebration of her birth."

The Queen immediately made a list of all the guests who would be invited to the christening. Among them were the little Princess's five fairy godmothers. The Queen did not know that, in her haste to send out the invitations, she had left one important person off the guest list. It was the Fairy Nightshade, and she was a very wicked fairy indeed.

"They will be sorry they did not ask me," she raged when she learned that she was the only person not invited. "I will give the baby a present she will never forget!"

The day of the christening dawned bright and clear. All the guests arrived for the party. Many had come from other countries. Never had there been such an array of silks and satins and coronets and jewels. Never had there been such a grand and happy occasion.

After the christening, each guest came up to the cradle and offered their gifts. There were silver spoons and mugs and little bracelets, as is the custom at a christening. There were grander gifts of diamonds and rubies and golden goblets. Each fairy godmother had a different kind of gift to offer the little princess.

"I will give her beauty," said the first.

"She will have from me the gift of cleverness," said the second.

"She will have a kind and merry heart," said the third.

"She will be rich, but her possessions will not spoil her," said the fourth. Before the fifth fairy could give her gift, there was a great commotion from the back of the hall.

"Who is there?" demanded the King. "Who dares to break in upon this important occasion?"

"The Fairy Nightshade," was the reply.

The Queen gave a little cry. "Oh dear, I forgot to ask her to the christening!"

She tried to put things right.

"Welcome, good fairy," she called. "Come in and join us."

A tall figure in a big, purple cloak came sweeping towards them. All of the guests stood aside nervously to let her pass.

"Thank you, your Majesty," said the Fairy Nightshade, approaching the cradle. The Queen noticed too late that the fairy had a cruel glint in her eye and a mocking smile upon her lips.

"So this is little Rose," said the Fairy Nightshade. "What a very pretty little baby she is! You will be glad to hear that I have not forgotten to bring her a gift."

"Thank you," said the Queen faintly.

"Your little daughter will become everything her godmothers have promised. She will be rich, happy, clever and kind-hearted. She will be the most beautiful girl in the kingdom. But when she is eighteen years old she will prick her finger on a spinning wheel needle and she will DIE!"

The wicked fairy's laughter echoed round the room. She bowed mockingly to the baby girl in the cradle and then turned on her heel and left the hall.

A stunned silence followed her. Then the Queen gave a little sob and took her baby into her arms.

"I can't let her die!" she cried, holding her close. "What shall we do?"

"You have forgotten that I haven't given her my gift," said a gentle voice at the Queen's elbow. It was the fifth fairy.

"I cannot remove the Fairy Nightshade's curse, but I can make things a little better. She will not die when she pricks her finger, but she will sleep for a hundred years."

"A hundred years!" cried the King. "But we will all be dead and buried by then!"

"No, your Majesty," went on the fifth fairy. "For you and all the kingdom will sleep with her. And when the hundred years have passed, someone will wake her with a kiss. At that moment, all of the people in your land will wake up and rub their eyes, as if they had only been asleep for a few hours."

"A hundred years' sleep is better than death," said the Queen, "but it is bad enough! We must see to it that the Princess never has the chance to see a needle. In that way we can avoid the curse."

The King immediately ordered that every needle and spinning wheel in the kingdom be destroyed. All the tailors, shoemakers and spinners left the country or

found other work. Anyone who needed new clothes or shoes ordered them to be sent from another land. And so, in this needleless kingdom, the little Princess Rose grew up. Everybody loved her, for she had received all the fairy godmothers' gifts. She was as kind and clever as she was beautiful. As her eighteenth birthday approached, the King began to plan her birthday party.

"I will ask every unmarried Prince and King to the party," he said. "For Princess Rose must think about choosing a husband."

"A husband!" cried Rose. "But I am happy enough without one. What if I do not care for any of the young men you have invited?"

The King smiled. "Oh, I'm sure you will find someone you like, my dear!"

The Princess sighed. "I only hope you are right, Father."

Rose was very worried. Although she was a good and obedient daughter, she did not want to make her parents unhappy by not marrying a prince of their choice; but to marry without love would be a very difficult thing to do. When the morning of her party arrived, she decided to get away from all the hustle and bustle and find a quiet corner of the palace where she could think about it all.

It seemed as if there was something happening in every room. In the kitchen, teams of cooks and kitchen maids were preparing for the party. In the bedrooms, all of the guests from distant countries were laying out their finery. In the ballroom, garlands of flowers were being used to decorate the fireplace and the chandeliers.

Princess Rose walked down corridors and up staircases. There was noise and fuss everywhere, and no peace anywhere. At last she came to a little, twisty staircase she had not noticed before.

"Surely I will find somewhere quiet up here," she said to herself. Up she went, until she came to a big, oak door. She pushed it open, and it squeaked on rusty hinges. The room was dim and dusty, but there was someone there. By the window the Princess could see an old woman hunched over a wheel.

She was about to turn round to go downstairs again, but she was curious. What was that wheel? She had never seen anything like it before. Very quietly, she crept forward.

"Hello, my dear," said the old woman, turning round. "Why, if it isn't the young Princess Rose!"

"What are you doing with that wheel?" asked the Princess.

"Why, spinning wool, my dear. Have you never seen anyone spinning wool before?"

"No," replied the Princess, for you will remember that the King had ordered all spinning wheels to be destroyed.

"It's very easy," said the old woman. "Why don't you sit down and try it yourself?"

"May I?"

Princess Rose did not see the cruel smile on the old woman's lips as she rose to her feet and let the young girl try her hand at spinning. For, of course, the old woman was the bad Fairy Nightshade in disguise!

"Oh, this is fun – it's so easy!" said the Princess as she turned the wheel. Then –

"Oh! I seem to have pricked my finger. Perhaps I'm not so good at this

[13]

after all. Here, sit down again. I ought to leave, anyway."

But when Princess Rose looked round, the old woman had completely vanished.

"Where has she gone? How strange! Well, I mustn't stop here to look for her. I do feel very tired suddenly."

The Princess left the attic room and went down the little, twisty staircase and along the palace corridors till she found her room. With each step she took, she grew slower and slower. When she reached her room, she staggered towards the bed and collapsed upon it. In seconds, she was fast asleep. Every room in the palace was suddenly silent. The cooks and kitchen maids in the kitchen fell asleep with their heads on the big kitchen table.

The servants in the ballroom sank down on the little, golden chairs and began to snore.

The party guests lay down upon their beds, half-dressed in their finery.

The King and Queen in the Throne Room sat with their heads slumped forward. The King's crown fell off his head and rolled across the floor.

Even the cats and dogs and horses fell fast asleep, as did the little mice in the stables and the outhouses.

And so they remained for one hundred years.

Time passed by. Weeds grew all over the palace gardens and the fountains and lakes dried up. Tiny saplings grew into tall trees. Around the palace walls a thick, thorny hedge grew, intertwined with roses. Soon, all that you could see of the palace were the turrets, peeping above the treetops. After fifty years you could not see the palace at all.

In far, distant kingdoms, many stories were told about the palace. It was said that once there had been a big party, and the guests had never returned home. A beautiful Princess and all of her family, friends and guests still remained in the mysterious palace, deep in an enchanted sleep. Many voyagers had returned with tales of a whole kingdom full of sleeping people, ruined houses and overgrown crops – a kingdom frozen in time.

A young Prince named Florian, had heard these stories from his grandfather, whose own parents had been guests at the eighteenth birthday party of the Princess Rose. They had never returned.

"The Princess had a rare beauty," said Prince Florian's grandfather. "She was kind, clever and lively. Every prince from every land sought her hand in marriage."

As Prince Florian grew from a boy into a good-looking young man, he could think of nothing but the tales of the hidden palace and the beautiful, sleeping Princess. When he was twenty years old, he decided that he would try to find the palace and solve the mystery. He took with him a sword which had been given to him by his grandfather. Its blade was sharp enough to defeat a thousand enemies or to cut through the trunk of the thickest tree.

Prince Florian journeyed for many months and for hundreds of miles. He knew when he had reached the borders of the sleeping kingdom, for his

journey became rougher and rougher. He fought his way through overgrown forests and thick, tangly undergrowth. Every now and again he would discover a sleeping peasant or a horse, standing upright between the shafts of a cart, but all were fast asleep.

At last Prince Florian came to a thorny hedge. It was so tall and so thick that he could see nothing through it, save the hundreds of pink roses that grew amongst its thorns. He set to work with his sword. He hacked at the thorns, until he had cleared a pathway through them. In spite of the sword's sharpness, it was a difficult task. The Prince's clothes were soon torn to shreds and his arms were covered in deep, ugly scratches. But at last, through the tangled branches, he could see the walls of a tall building.

"I have found the hidden palace!" Prince Florian cried. He plucked a rose from the thorny hedge as he pushed his way through the last of it. Minutes later, he was standing by the great wooden door. Its hinges and bars were tarnished green, and its key was so rusty that the Prince doubted if he could turn it. He tried with all his strength, and at last the key turned in the lock. The great gate swung open, and the Prince's eyes widened in wonder. Everywhere he saw sleeping servants and dogs and horses. As he walked through the courtyard to the main entrance, he found footmen lying across his path, and little servant girls curled up asleep in cobwebbed corners. Prince Florian glanced into many rooms. He found the Throne Room where the King and Queen were, and he picked up the King's crown and laid it gently beside him. Then on he went, up the grand staircase, until at last he found the room where the Princess Rose was sleeping.

"Oh!" breathed the Prince. He was looking down upon the loveliest girl he had ever set eyes on. She lay with her hair spread across the pillow like a curtain. She was smiling in her sleep, as though she was about to wake at any moment. Prince Florian could not resist it. He bent over the bed and kissed her tenderly on the cheek.

Immediately the Princess opened her eyes and blinked at the young man who was bending over her.

"Oh, I've had such a lovely sleep," she yawned. "But I must get up now. It's my birthday, you see, and I'm to have a party. If you will excuse me saying so, you look a bit scruffy for a guest."

But she smiled warmly at Prince Florian all the same.

He helped her to her feet and began to explain to her about her hundred years' sleep and his quest to find her.

Her eyes did not leave his face. When he reached the bit about the thorny hedge, she reached out and touched the scratches on his arm.

"You did this for me?" she said. "Oh, do forgive me for saying you looked scruffy. I will see to it that your arm is bandaged and that you have new clothes immediately."

When she rang for a servant, one appeared instantly. The Prince's kiss had removed the wicked fairy's spell, as the fifth fairy had said it would. Everyone in the palace was now awake. The cobwebs and dust vanished, as if they had never been, and the palace gardens lay spick and span in the sunshine. Everyone busied themselves preparing for the Princess's eighteenth birthday party.

The Princess herself now had no worries about choosing a suitable Prince for her husband. She had already made up her mind who that man would be!

Prince Florian and Princess Rose were married the following month on a bright summer's day when all was right with the world. Nightshade was furious that her curse was lifted at last. She packed her bags and left the kingdom, never to be seen again. And when later the happy young couple's first son was born, there was no fear that the bad fairy would spoil *his* christening.

HANSEL AND GRETEL

LONG ago, on the edge of a deep forest, a woodcutter lived with his wife and two children, Hansel and Gretel. The woodcutter was a kind, gentle man, but he was very afraid of his wife who had no kindness in her.

One year there was a big famine, and the family had very little food.

"What shall we do, Wife?" asked the woodcutter one evening, after the children had gone to bed.

"If the children stay here, we will all starve," said his wife. "But if we send them off into the forest, then we at least will have enough to eat."

The woodcutter was horrified. "We can't get rid of our own children!"

"You are too soft-hearted," snapped the wife. "They are quite old enough to look after themselves."

The woodcutter knew that the children would probably be eaten by wild animals in the forest, but he was too afraid of his wife's anger to say no. He told her that he would take the children off into the forest the next morning.

But Hansel and Gretel had crept out of bed and had heard every word. Gretel put her arm round Hansel and sobbed.

"Don't worry, Gretel," said Hansel. "We won't get lost in the forest. Just leave it to me."

When his parents had gone to bed, Hansel crept out into the yard and picked up a big handful of little, white stones.

The next morning, the children's mother told them to go off into the forest with their father to help him cut wood. She gave them some white bread for their lunch.

"That is the last piece of food in the house," she grumbled. "Goodness knows what will become of us."

As the woodcutter and the children set off from home, Hansel lagged behind.

"What's the matter?" asked his father. "Why do you keep looking back?"

"I'm saying goodbye to my little cat," said Hansel. "Look, there she is, sitting on the fence!"

"Well, hurry along," said the woodcutter. He felt more and more unhappy about leaving his children, and he wanted the parting to be over as quickly as possible.

They walked on and on until they reached a clearing in the very deepest part of the forest.

"Now be good, children, and stay here until I get back," said the woodcutter.

Gretel started to cry, but Hansel whispered to her. "Don't worry, Gretel. Didn't you see me turning round? I was leaving a trail of little, white stones so that we can follow it home." With tears in his eyes, the woodcutter hugged Hansel and Gretel.

"Keep safe," he said. He then hurried away without looking back.

The children ate their bread and rested a little.

"Wait until nightfall," said Hansel. "Then we will be able to see the white stones gleaming in the moonlight."

At last the sunlight faded and the moon rose – and there were the stones, shining like a path through the trees.

It did not take Hansel and Gretel long to find their way home again. Their father was just locking up for the night. He cried out with joy when he saw them coming towards the cottage. Their mother, though, was furious.

"Didn't I tell you to take them so far that they would never find their way back?" she muttered to the woodcutter.

The woodcutter was very happy to have his children home with him again. He would not agree to take them back into the forest the next day, especially since his wife had managed to scrape together a little more bread, and oats for porridge. It was not long, though, before they ran out of food again. Once again the woodcutter's wife told him to take Hansel and Gretel back into the forest.

"And see that you lose them for good this time," she added. Poor Hansel could not pick up any more white stones because his mother had locked both children in for the night.

"Don't worry, I will think of something else," he told Gretel.

The next morning their mother gave them two crusts of white bread. Hansel crumbled his up into little pieces. Once more, he walked along behind.

"Come on, Hansel," said the woodcutter. "Why do you keep looking back?"

"I can see a little, white bird sitting on the roof," said Hansel. "She is singing so prettily!"

Of course he was really scattering a trail of white crumbs through the forest so that he and Gretel could find their way home again.

Once again they reached the little clearing, and once more, their father said goodbye to them.

Gretel was impatient to set off home again, but Hansel told her that they must wait until the moon rose.

"Then we will be able to see the crumbs," he said.

It seemed a very long day. Hansel and Gretel had to share one piece of bread between them. By the time the sun had set, they were both very hungry.

The birds had been hungry too! They had eaten every crumb that Hansel had left on the path. Now the children could not follow the trail and were quite lost. They could not see where they were going, but they knew they must try to find shelter and food somewhere. They began to follow a little winding path through the trees. They walked on until daybreak. By then, they were both so tired and hungry that they could barely go a step further.

"Hansel!" Gretel suddenly cried. "Look! Isn't that a little cottage ahead of us?"

The sight of the cottage made them feel better. They began to run towards it. They stopped on the edge of a little, grassy clearing and stared. They could hardly believe their eyes.

"It *is* a cottage!" cried Hansel. "And it's made of gingerbread!"

"It has barley-sugar windows and cakes for tiles!" gasped Gretel. "Do you think the owner will mind if we eat some of it?"

They were good, honest children who would never steal from anyone. They were so very hungry, though, that they could not stop themselves from nibbling a piece off the walls and breaking a barley-sugar window.

"WHO'S THAT EATING MY HOUSE?"

The children dropped the pieces of cake and sugar in fright. An old, old woman had opened the door and was standing there, smiling at them.

"You poor dears," she said. "How tired and hungry you look. You must have been lost in the forest. Well, come on in and have some breakfast."

She took Gretel by the hand. "Come with me, little girl. There's plenty of food inside."

Their father had always told them not to talk to strangers, but the old lady looked so kind that Hansel and Gretel followed her into her little cottage. A wonderful meal was laid out on a big table – pancakes with cream and honey, new bread with rich yellow butter, and every kind of sweet and cake you could think of.

Hansel and Gretel sat down and ate until they were completely full. It was the best food they had ever tasted.

"You must be very tired," the old woman said when they had finished eating. "I have two little beds that are all made up and ready for you to sleep in."

And sure enough, upstairs were two blue-painted beds with snowy-white sheets and patchwork blankets. Hansel and Gretel each climbed into a bed and were soon fast asleep.

Now the old woman was not kind and caring at all. She was a wicked witch who captured little children and fattened them up for her supper. While Hansel and Gretel slept in their beds, the old witch crept into the room, roughly grabbed Hansel and carried him downstairs before he knew what was happening.

Gretel was awake by now. She leapt out of bed and ran down the stairs and out into the yard. The old witch was pushing Hansel into a big iron-barred cage.

Gretel grabbed hold of the witch's arm.

"What are you doing to him? Let him out! Why are you locking him away?"

The old witch cackled, and she grinned a black-toothed smile as she shook her arm free.

"You silly little children! Did you really think I would feed you for nothing? Your brother is tender and young. He's a bit skinny; but once he's fattened up, he'll be just right for the cooking pot."

Hansel was awake by now and looking through the bars of the cage. He thought he was in the middle of a bad dream. He saw Gretel's

frightened face, and the old woman laughing cruelly at the thought of the good meal she would have once he was fat enough.

"Come along, girl," the old witch snapped at Gretel. "There's a pile of work to be done. I want this floor swept and polished to begin with – and then you can get lunch for your brother."

It did not take Gretel long to learn that, while Hansel was to be fed fine food until he was fat enough to eat, she would have only crusts and water.

Several days passed. Gretel would take Hansel his lunch of chicken stew, and sometimes, if the old witch was not looking, her brother would pass some of the food back to her through the bars. He kept the bones of the chicken so that when the witch came to the cage to see how fat he was, he could stick out a chicken bone instead of his finger.

"Hm," said the old witch. "You're still very skinny. I'll give you just a week. If you're still skin and bones by then, I'll eat you anyway."

Hansel was very scared indeed when Gretel took him his next meal.

"What can I do, Gretel?" he asked. "You heard what the old witch said. She will eat me at the end of the week, even if I'm not fat enough."

"Don't worry, Hansel," said Gretel. "I won't let you be eaten. I'll think of something."

By Friday, the witch had decided to eat Hansel. She woke Gretel early and made her prepare the cooking pot and knead the bread.

"A nice lot of onions and carrots," she said. "I like my boys served up with vegetables."

Gretel did as the witch asked. 'I must think of some way to save Hansel,' she thought.

"Now light the oven," ordered the old witch.

Gretel opened the door of the oven and lit it.

"We'll bake the bread first," said the witch. "But first, I want you to climb into the oven to see if it is hot enough."

Of course, the old witch meant to slam the door on Gretel so that she would be cooked too.

Gretel stared at the flames inside the oven.

"You must think I am very stupid," she said, "but I cannot see how I should climb in. It seems very small for a big girl like me."

The witch gave an impatient sigh. "Stupid girl!" she shrieked. "Here's how you do it."

And pushing Gretel aside, she showed Gretel how to climb into the oven. This was Gretel's chance! She gave the witch one big push, and the wicked old woman fell forward, right into the flames.

Gretel quickly slammed the door. When she was quite sure that the witch could not climb out again, she ran into the yard and let Hansel out of his iron cage.

"The old witch is dead!" she cried. They both hugged each other and danced for joy.

More happiness was to come. When Hansel and Gretel looked round the cottage, they found chests of precious jewels and gold. They filled their pockets with as much as they could carry. Then they left the gingerbread cottage and set off through the big, dark forest. They hoped that they could find their way home again.

They walked and walked until they reached a big, wide river that flowed through the forest. There was no bridge across it, and the two children stood on the bank, wondering what to do. Suddenly, a duck swam by.

"Dear, kind, duck, could we cross the water on your back?" they called out to him.

"Of course," quacked the duck. "Climb aboard."

Gretel hitched up her skirt and climbed on to the duck's broad back, and Hansel climbed up beside her.

As soon as they reached the other bank, the children knew where they were.

"Our cottage is just along this little path," cried Gretel, running forward. However Hansel hung back.

"Do you think our mother will be cross with us?"

They were both very scared of her.

"Father will be glad to see us at least," said Gretel. They both ran and danced along the little path towards home as fast as they could.

And of course their father *was* glad to see them. He could hardly believe his eyes.

"I thought you had been eaten by wild animals," he cried as he put his arms around them both.

"We were nearly eaten by a witch," laughed Gretel. "But we soon got rid of *her*."

Their father took them inside and told them that their mother was dead. They could not feel very sad about it. She had never been kind to them.

"And the famine is over!" said the woodcutter. "There's plenty to eat again."

So Hansel and Gretel and the woodcutter all lived happily together in the little cottage at the edge of the forest. No one knew what became of the gingerbread house. Perhaps some child, lost in the forest, ate it all up!

RAPUNZEL

THERE once was a couple, who longed for a child from the moment they were first married. Many years passed, but no child was born and the wife grew more and more unhappy.

"All my friends have children," she said. "I am the only one without a child to love and care for."

The couple lived next to a beautiful garden which was owned by an old witch. In it the witch grew many herbs; among them was a herb known as rapunzel.

One day the wife said to her husband, "I just fancy a salad made of rapunzel leaves. Go into the witch's garden and fetch me some."

The man was afraid, for everyone around was terrified of the witch and kept well away from her. But his wife nagged at him so much that at last he crept into the garden and picked a large bunch of rapunzel leaves.

His wife ate them greedily. They were delicious. No sooner had she finished them than she wanted more.

Her husband quaked with fear, but he knew his wife would not rest until she had more of the tasty herb. She had grown very bad-tempered and

bossy over the years. So back he went as soon as darkness fell. He was just picking the rapunzel leaves when a bony hand fell on his shoulder.

"Ha! I've caught you red-handed, you thief! Well now, what spell shall I put on you to punish you for your crime?"

"Oh, please don't harm me," pleaded the man. "My wife sent me into your garden because she loves eating your rapunzel."

The old witch smiled craftily.

"Your wife may have as many rapunzel leaves as she wants," she said. "But there is one condition."

"What is that?"

"You must give me the child she will bear."

'Since my wife cannot have children,' thought the man, 'I have escaped lightly.' But when he returned to the cottage, his wife greeted him with a happy smile.

"Have you picked the rapunzel leaves?" she asked eagerly. "For now I need enough food for two – I am expecting a child, Husband. Isn't that wonderful news!"

With a heavy heart, the man told his wife all that had happened in the witch's garden. She wept bitterly and pleaded with her husband to go back to the witch again, taking the stolen rapunzel leaves with him. But the witch laughed in his face, and he could do nothing to make her take back her demands for their newborn child.

As soon as the baby was born, the witch came knock-knocking at their door.

"I've come for the baby," she said. The wife turned pale and held her little daughter to her breast.

"Come on now," said the witch. "I can use my magic to steal her away, but it's as well if you give her to me yourself. What do you call her?"

"Her name is Rapunzel," she told the witch, "after the herb that we stole from your garden. Please look after her well."

The witch took the sleeping child into her arms and hurried across to her own house, locking and barring the door behind her.

The years went by, and the witch did indeed look after Rapunzel well. The baby grew into a pretty little girl with long, golden hair. The witch never let her play outside for fear of her parents snatching her back again. As she grew from a little child into a beautiful young girl, the witch was

even more determined that Rapunzel should not escape from her. One day she took her many miles from the house and shut her up in a tall tower with no staircase and no door. She would visit Rapunzel each day and to enter the tower the old witch would stand and call up to her:

"Rapunzel, Rapunzel, let down your golden hair."

And Rapunzel would unwind her hair and let her loose tresses hang from the window. Then the witch would climb up them into her room.

Several years passed and Rapunzel grew even more beautiful. And still the old witch would not let the poor girl out of her tall prison. One day, a young prince was riding by and he heard the sound of sweet singing. It was coming from the very top of the high tower. The prince was puzzled. If there was someone up there, how did she get there? There was no door at the foot of the tower and when he looked through a window, he saw no staircase. He wanted so much to find out who sang so sweetly, high up above him. For the moment, he could do nothing, so he mounted his horse and turned home. But he could not forget the beautiful singing. He came back time after time to try to catch a glimpse of the owner of the voice. Then one day, as he stood looking up at the tower, he heard the sound of footsteps approaching. Quickly, he hid behind a tree. An ugly old witch appeared and shouted up to the singing voice:

"Rapunzel, Rapunzel, let down your golden hair."

The prince stood quietly by the tree, wondering what would happen next. As he looked upwards, he saw a beautiful girl unwinding her golden hair and tossing it down to the old witch. The witch climbed up it like a rope.

'So that's the staircase to the tower,' he thought. 'Well, the witch may be able to climb up, but the poor girl cannot climb down. I must see if I can rescue her.'

The following evening, as the sun dipped down behind the tall tower, the prince tied his horse to a tree, and called up to the singing voice:

"Rapunzel, Rapunzel, let down your golden hair."

At the top of the tower, Rapunzel stopped singing, and listened. It was not the witch calling up to her. Since the poor girl had no friends and no companion other than the witch, she wondered who the voice belonged to. With beating heart, Rapunzel unwound her hair and let it down from the window.

Whoever would climb up it?

As soon as the prince reached the window-ledge, Rapunzel turned around. She had never seen a man before, and the sight of the handsome young stranger who stood in front of her made her heart beat even faster.

"How is it that you are imprisoned here all alone?" asked the prince. Rapunzel told him of how she was brought up by the witch, who allowed her no friends and had kept her in the tower for many years.

Now the prince had fallen in love with Rapunzel the moment he had set eyes upon her.

"I will rescue you from this dreary tower and take you back to my palace," he said. And he knew in his heart that he would marry this sweet maiden once she had escaped the clutches of the old witch.

As for Rapunzel, the grim, grey tower was suddenly bathed in golden light as the young prince smiled at her. She would go away and never see the old witch, or the tower again. And perhaps one day she may even marry this handsome young man who looked at her so tenderly.

But then she frowned.

"How can I escape from the tower? I cannot climb down by my own hair. I need a ladder . . ."

They both thought and thought until they came up with a plan.

The prince promised that he would visit her every evening after the witch had left her. Each time he came, he would bring a long thread of silk. From this Rapunzel would weave a long silken ladder.

Of course, all this took time. As usual, the witch came each day to Rapunzel's tower. At first she suspected nothing. But one day, as she pulled herself up by Rapunzel's hair, the girl said to her without thinking, "You do feel heavy, good mother. The prince is so much lighter than you!"

The witch sprang into the room and glared angrily. Too late, Rapunzel realised what she had said.

"You wicked child!" screamed the witch. "You have been deceiving me. You have allowed a young man into this tower where I have looked after you so carefully."

She was so angry that she snatched hold of Rapunzel's beautiful golden hair and cut it from her head.

"So you want to leave the tower, do you?" she said. "Well, you shall do

so – but not with your handsome prince! Oh no, I shall see to it that you will never see him again."

The witch hung the golden tresses from the window, threw Rapunzel over her shoulder, and climbed down to the bottom of the tower. Then she pulled down the golden hair, and kept it safely in her bag.

"Please let me go, dear mother!" pleaded Rapunzel. The witch took no notice and dragged her all through the forest to a lonely barren spot where she left the weeping girl to look after herself.

"So now you have freedom," cackled the witch. "Just see how you like it!"

The witch returned to the tower and lay in wait for the prince. Very soon she heard his voice calling out from below:

"Rapunzel, Rapunzel, let down your golden hair."

The witch held on to the tresses and tossed the other end down to the prince.

"Now come on up, my lovely," she said softly. "And see what you will find here."

The prince climbed into the room. The smile died on his face as he saw the old witch instead of his beloved Rapunzel.

"What have you done with her?" he cried.

"Aha, the pretty bird has flown. She will not sing any longer, for the cat has caught her. And the cat will scratch out your eyes too."

The prince was mad with grief. Without thinking, he threw himself from the tower so that he could escape from the witch's mocking cries.

"You will never see Rapunzel again," she called to him as he fell down. He landed in some thorny bushes at the foot of the tower. He escaped with his life, but the wicked thorns from the bushes pierced his eyes, and he found that he was blind.

Although the prince no longer had his sight, he never gave up hope of finding his beloved Rapunzel again. For months and years he wandered all round the kingdom, looking for her.

At long last, the prince came to the very place where the witch had left Rapunzel. It was a wild and deserted spot, but the girl had made herself a little home which she shared with the wild animals. She was as beautiful as ever, and each day she would cheer herself up by singing a song.

And it was then that the poor, blind prince, riding through the barren countryside, suddenly heard her sweet singing. He recognised the voice immediately and sprang from his horse.

"Rapunzel!" he cried.

Rapunzel looked up and saw her dear prince running sightlessly towards her.

"What has happened to you?" she cried. "Your poor, poor eyes!"

She threw her arms around his neck and wept with joy and pity. And as she wept, two of her tears fell onto his eyes, and his sight returned.

The prince could hardly believe that he could see again at last.

"I never thought I would look on your lovely face again," he told Rapunzel. And taking her by the hand, he led her back to his father's palace, where everyone greeted them with great joy. Their beloved prince was blind no longer, and he had brought back with him a lovely bride.

The two of them were soon married, and they lived together in great happiness, far away from the wicked witch's clutches.

"Your orders are as before," he said. "All this must be turned to gold before morning, or you die!"

The miller's daughter sat at the wheel helplessly, turning it round and round. She tried to spin some straw with it, but of course nothing happened.

She put her head in her hands and cried bitterly.

Once more the door opened, and once more the little man came into the room.

"Crying again?" he asked. "Don't tell me that the King wants even more gold!"

The miller's daughter nodded her head silently.

"Very well," said the little man briskly. "Let me take your place, and I will do as before. But I need payment."

The girl pulled a ring off her finger.

"Take this," she said. "It is all I have left."

The little man pocketed the ring and sat down at the wheel. Very soon, it was whirring away merrily. The piles of straw vanished, and golden thread took its place.

By dawn the task was completed.

"Oh, thank you!" cried the girl, clapping her hands. But the little man had already disappeared.

"Very good," said the King later, rubbing his hands with joy. "But can you do it again? If you can, then you will certainly become my Queen. But if not – "

'I will die,' thought the girl, hopelessly. That night the King took her to a third room filled with straw and locked the door.

As soon as the girl sat down at the wheel, the little man appeared for the third time. Goodness knows how he had come into the room, with the door locked!

This time the miller's daughter felt no joy at his appearance.

"I have nothing left to give you," she said. "So I suppose you will not help me."

"I will help you," said the little man. "But in return you must make me a promise."

"Oh, anything you wish!" cried the miller's daughter.

"You must promise me that when you become Queen you will give me your first child."

The miller's daughter did not like the sound of this, but it was a choice between giving the little man her promise or dying. 'And who knows,' she thought, 'the King may not marry me, and I may never become Queen.'

So she promised to give her first-born child to the little man. He sat down at the wheel and spun the gold as he had done before.

"Don't forget your promise," he called as he left her.

The King now had enough gold to keep him happy for a while. 'I will marry the miller's daughter,' he thought. 'For nowhere in the kingdom will I be able to find such a rich wife!'

The couple were soon married, and the miller's daughter became Queen. The years passed by, and soon she forgot all about the little man who had saved her life and demanded a promise. She gave birth to a fine son, and for a while she and the King were very happy.

Then one fine day as she sat rocking the baby's cradle, the door opened, and the little man suddenly appeared.

The young Queen stared at him.

"Why are you here?" she asked. "What do you want?"

"Have you forgotten me already?" asked the little man. "Have you forgotten your promise?"

The Queen's face turned pale. She took her little son into her arms.

"Oh no, you cannot have my son," she cried. "I can give you all the jewels and riches you want now, for I am no longer poor. But I cannot give you my son."

"A promise is a promise," snapped the little man. "I want your son, and nothing else will do. But I tell you what. If you can guess my name in three days, then I will forget your promise, and you will be able to keep your son."

Three days! The Queen knew that she must act quickly. She sent messengers all over the kingdom to ask if anyone could tell her the name of the little man. In the meanwhile, he returned to her each day, and she tried guessing herself.

"Is it Shortlegs?"

"No," laughed the little man.

"Longnose?"

"No!"

"Bigears?"

"No! No! No!" And the little man hopped and skipped out of the Palace, laughing as he went.

"I shall soon have the King's son! I shall soon have the Prince!"

Well, the Queen began to think of all the names under the sun. She thought of magical names, christian names, and animal names. But each time she tried a list of new names, the little man danced round the room and cried, "No, no, that is not my name!"

And now it was the end of the second day, and the Queen was no nearer finding out his name.

On the morning of the third day, one of the Queen's messengers appeared. He was out of breath and sore-footed.

"Madam," he said. "I have found out where the little man lives. If you saddle your horse quickly we can ride there, and you may well discover his name."

The Queen saddled up her horse, and they rode off through the forest till they came to a clearing where a little cottage stood. It was no bigger than a doll's house.

"Come behind this tree," whispered the messenger. "You may learn something."

Almost at once, the little man came out of the cottage and began to dance in circles round the clearing, singing,

"*Is it Shortlegs, is it Tom?*
Is it Pusskins, Sam or John?
Is it Caspar, Greencoat, Sam?
No, No, No, your little man
Has beaten you at the guessing game,
For RUMPELSTILTSKIN IS MY NAME!"

The Queen gave a little gasp of delight. She had found out what she wanted! She mounted her horse and galloped back to the Palace, murmuring his name as she went, in case she should forget it.

That evening, the little man came to the Palace for the last time.

"One more guess, your Majesty!" he gloated. "After that, your son shall be mine!"

"Now let me see," began the Queen. "Could it possibly be – could it be – RUMPELSTILTSKIN!"

The little man gave a great cry of rage.

"Somebody must have told you!" he screamed. And he stamped on the floor so hard that he disappeared right through it and was never seen again.

CINDERELLA

CINDERELLA had not always been her name. Long ago, before her mother died, she had a pretty name, but she had long forgotten what it was. Her father had married again, and his new wife had brought her own two girls to live with them.

It was these two girls, Griselda and Gudrun, who had unkindly named their step-sister Cinderella.

"It's a very good name," said Gudrun, sneering, "since you spend all your time sweeping out the grate."

For the girls and their mother saw to it that Cinderella worked hard all day, sweeping and cleaning the house. They were jealous of her, for she was so much prettier than they were. Because they were lazy and vain, Gudrun and Griselda did not help Cinderella with her tasks. When their stepfather came home from work, they would pretend they had done all the work themselves.

"Don't you think the house is as clean as a new pin?" Griselda said to him. "We worked ever so hard to make it nice for you, didn't we, Gudrun?"

"Yes," said Gudrun. 'We're not like that lazy daughter of yours, who just sits dreaming all day."

Cinderella's father was too afraid of his new wife and her daughters to ask why his own daughter looked so drab and dusty and tired, while Griselda and Gudrun were always dressed in the latest fashion, with hands so fine and white that he knew they never did any hard work.

One day, while Cinderella was sweeping the kitchen floor and polishing the tiles, Gudrun and Griselda swept into the room, overturning Cinderella's pail of water.

"Oh dear, I'm *so* sorry," cried Gudrun, laughing and swilling the water round the floor. "But we're *so* excited, aren't we, Griselda?"

Griselda was waving a big, important-looking white card.

"What's that?" asked Cinderella, trying to see what the card said. Griselda snatched it away from her.

"Oh, it's not for you, little sister. It's an invitation to the Prince's Ball. Fancy that! He wants us, Griselda and Gudrun, to attend!"

The invitation had been for all three daughters, but the girls were not going to let Cinderella know that.

"Wasn't I invited too?" asked Cinderella.

"Of course not! What a thought! You in your dusty rags! Why, you would have nothing suitable to wear for it."

Cinderella knew this was true. She had only the clothes she worked in. Every bit of money Cinderella's father gave for the girls' clothes was spent on Griselda and Gudrun. Cinderella sighed and began to mop up all the water Gudrun had spilled over the floor.

"Come on," said Griselda impatiently. "Let's go to our room, sister, and plan what we'll wear."

"They say the Prince is looking for a wife," said Gudrun. "He may choose me!"

"What makes you think that?" said Griselda spitefully. "You're too fat, and you have squinty eyes."

"That's better than being tall and skinny and having big feet," snapped Gudrun.

So you see, the two girls weren't very kind to each other either. They flounced out of the kitchen and left Cinderella alone.

Cinderella sat on her little stool by the fireside and gazed dreamily into the flames.

'How wonderful it would be to go to the Ball,' she thought. 'I've never been inside the palace. They say it is very grand. But there's no use in dreaming. I can't go, and that is that! I might as well forget all about it.'

It was difficult for Cinderella to forget all about it, though, because Griselda and Gudrun kept bursting into the kitchen and dancing in front of her.

"What do you think of this gown, Cinders?" asked Griselda. "Is it not the most wonderful green? It's *the* most fashionable colour this year, you know."

Then in would come Gudrun.

"Green doesn't suit you," she cried. "You look just like Jack's beanstalk!" She swirled in front of Cinderella in a wave of pink chiffon.

"And *you* look like a sickly meringue!" retorted Griselda.

Cinderella thought they both looked awful, but she was too polite to say so.

"I'm sure the Prince will notice you at once," she said.

On the night of the Ball, Cinderella's father came down into the kitchen.

"Still working, Cinders?" he asked. "Aren't you going to the Ball?"

Cinderella shook her head.

"No, Father," she said. "I'm not a girl who likes big, grand Balls. I will wait here for you all, and hear all about it when you get back."

Her father shook his head. "What a pity," he said. "The Prince would have noticed you at once. You are prettier than any other girl in this city, you know."

He kissed her goodbye and hurried away upstairs to where his wife and two stepdaughters were impatiently waiting for him. Cinderella heard the clatter of the coach and horses as they drove off.

The house was completely silent once the sound of the horses' hooves had died away. Only the tick-tock of the grandfather clock could be heard at the top of the stairs, and the occasional scamperings and squeakings of mice as they stole out of their mousehole into the kitchen. If you listened very carefully, you would hear a tiny sob and a sigh. For, try as she may, Cinderella could not forget the Ball.

"They'll be arriving just now," she said to herself. "I wonder what the Grand Ballroom looks like? I wonder what the Prince will be wearing?"

Once, long ago, Cinderella had seen the Prince and thought he looked handsome and kind. How she would have loved to have met him!

But now it was too late. She would never go to the Ball. How could she go anywhere when she had only rags to wear? Cinderella put down her broom and sat on her stool by the fire. Two tears trickled down her cheeks, and before she could stop herself, she was crying her heart out.

"Come, come, child! This won't do!"

Cinderella looked up. Through her tears she saw a tall, beautiful lady standing beside her. She was dressed in blue, and her face shone with kindness and concern.

"Who are you?" asked Cinderella. "I didn't hear anyone come in. What are you doing here?"

The tall lady smiled. "Long ago, when your mother was still alive, you were christened; and as was usual in those days, you were given a Fairy Godmother."

Cinderella wiped her eyes on her dusty sleeve and stared hard at the lady.

"You are my Fairy Godmother? Can this be true? Why, I never knew I had anyone in the world but my own father."

The Fairy Godmother laid her hand gently on Cinderella's shoulder.

"If there's anyone who needs a Fairy Godmother now, it's you," she said. "I've been watching this house. I've seen how unkindly you are treated by your two stepsisters. I know how much you long to go to the Ball."

At the mention of the Ball, Cinderella began to cry again.

"But you can see, Fairy Godmother, that I can't possibly go. I have no other clothes than what I am wearing now."

"But that's why I've come! I can make all things possible."

The Fairy Godmother drew out a silver wand from under her cloak and waved it three times round Cinderella's head. There was a blinding flash. Cinderella stood up and slowly looked down at what she was wearing. Gone was her dirty old dress with the patches and torn hem. In its place was a fine, white, silk ballgown, embroidered with gold thread. As her tears dried on her cheeks, Cinderella slowly twirled round. The dress billowed and shimmered with a thousand lights. On her feet she wore slippers of crystal. She put her hand to her head and drew off a little diamond coronet.

"Oh, Fairy Godmother," she cried. "I look like a Princess!"

"You always have," said her Fairy Godmother. "And you've kept yourself hidden for too long. Now it is time to show yourself at the Ball!"

Everything was happening too quickly. Cinderella's mind was in a whirl.

"How will I get there?" she asked. "I'm so grateful for what you have done that I don't like to mention it – but everyone goes to the Prince's Ball in a carriage."

"I said I could make all things possible," said the Fairy Godmother. She strode to the kitchen door and out into the yard. Minutes later she reappeared with two squirming frogs in her hand. Once more she drew out her wand and waved it. In a flash of light, the frogs disappeared. Instead, two footmen stood there, all dressed up in green velvet and gold braid.

"You'll need a coach, of course," said Cinderella's Fairy Godmother, "and four horses."

By now Cinderella knew that her Fairy Godmother could arrange anything. She was not surprised when a pumpkin from the yard was changed into a golden coach, and four little mice from the scullery became a team of splendid white horses with green and gold leather trappings. Cinderella was now ready for the Ball!

Laughing happily, she ran out into the yard. A footman helped her into the coach.

"Not so fast," said her Fairy Godmother. "Just wait a moment and listen to what I have to say, for this is important."

Cinderella leaned out of the coach, her mind racing ahead of her to the Palace and all the wonderful things she would see there.

"Whatever you do, you must leave the Ball by midnight. If you are but one second late, the footmen, the coach, and the horses will all disappear and become as they were before they were enchanted. And you, my dear, will become poor, little Cinders again, with your ragged dress and dirty hands."

"I'll remember," said Cinderella, as the coach left the yard and galloped off down the street towards the palace. The dim figure of her Fairy Godmother faded from sight.

In the Palace Ballroom, the Prince was standing at the foot of the stairs, greeting each guest as they walked down.

It was a pity that Gudrun tripped up over her ballgown as she reached the Prince. He was very polite as he smiled and helped her to her feet.

"You see, sister," she said to Griselda later. "He smiled at me!"

"Laughed, more like," said Griselda, feeling angry. The Prince had barely looked at her in her bright green gown. "What is happening? Why hasn't the music started? All the guests have arrived."

"There seems to be one more," said Cinderella's father quietly. "Look, she is coming down the stairs now."

Every head in the ballroom turned towards the beautiful girl who was walking slowly down the grand staircase to the Prince. Her face shone with a light that matched the thousand glittering threads in her silk dress and the diamond coronet in her hair.

"Just our luck!" whispered Griselda to her mother. "What hope have we that the Prince will dance with either of us now? You can see he is quite besotted with her."

"Who is she?" wondered Gudrun. "I cannot remember ever seeing her before."

Everyone in the room was saying the same thing. How could such a beautiful girl stay hidden?

"Who are you?" the Prince asked Cinderella as he waltzed round the room with her. "What is your name?"

'If I tell him I am Cinderella, he will want to know how I came by such a name,' she thought to herself. 'I do not want to spoil his happiness by telling him that I'm only a kitchen maid.'

"I will tell you at the end of the Ball," she said, smiling up at him. "But now you must dance with your other guests."

For a short time he left her, but wherever they were in the room, they would turn to smile at each other. The evening flew by like the wind. All too soon, it was the last dance. The Prince chose Cinderella as his partner. They waltzed round and round, and Cinderella's heart sang with happiness. She forgot her drab life, she even forgot her Fairy Godmother. She only knew that she loved the Prince and that he loved her. The big clock at the head of the stairs began to strike midnight.

One, two, three . . .

"Now you must tell me your name," said the Prince.

Her name! Oh no, she couldn't! And suddenly Cinderella remembered her kitchen, her little stool, and her Fairy Godmother who had made all this happen. And she remembered what the good fairy had said as she left for the palace!

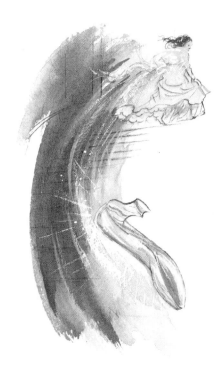

Cinderella suddenly pulled her hand away from the Prince.

"I must go," she cried. "I have stayed too long – please, I must hurry!"

She turned and ran up the big staircase to the door. As she went, she tripped, and one of her little crystal slippers fell off. She would have to leave it. She had no time . . .

The clock was chiming the last stroke of midnight as Cinderella ran out of the door. And as she breathed the cold night air, she saw in front of her not the coach and horses, but a very large pumpkin, sitting in the driveway. A couple of frogs hopped off into the bushes, and four mice scuttled away into the darkness.

Cinderella stopped running. She ran her hands over her thin little dress with the patches on it. She put her hand to her head and felt only her tangly, untidy hair. Everything had happened just as her Fairy Godmother had said it would. Shivering with the cold, she ran down the drive and slipped out by the big gates before the guards could stop her.

"Well, that's that," she said to herself as she crept home. "I was so happy to be at the Ball. But now it's all over, and I don't expect I shall ever set eyes on my Prince again."

But she was wrong.

Back at the palace, the Prince was puzzled and upset. He could not understand why his beautiful partner had fled from him. He picked up her slipper on the stair and held it to his heart.

"Such a tiny foot," he said. "There cannot be another like it in the kingdom."

It gave him an idea. "I will find her," he vowed. "Every noble girl in the land shall try on the slipper. And when the slipper fits the foot perfectly, I will have found my lovely princess!"

Cinderella reached home before the rest of the family arrived. She opened the door to them and listened to the chattering of her two sisters as they described the Ball, and the beautiful stranger who had won the Prince's heart.

"She might be beautiful," said Griselda, "but what a way to behave! Why, she practically pushed him to the ground, she was so eager to get away from him."

"*I* wouldn't have behaved like that," said Gudrun smugly. "I would have stayed with him for ever."

"Huh!" said Griselda. "Then it would be the Prince who would want to escape."

"She left her slipper behind," said the girls' mother. "He wants every noble girl in the land to try it on. When it fits perfectly, he will have found his bride."

The very next day, the messenger began his long task of finding the owner of the crystal slipper.

"When will he come here?" asked Gudrun impatiently.

"Do you think your big, fat foot will fit the slipper?" sneered her sister. "Now mine is nice and slim – "

"Bony," said Gudrun. "And you have terrible corns."

At long last there was a loud and important knock at the door. Both sisters screamed with excitement and ran to open it.

The messenger looked at them doubtfully.

"If I may say so, your feet look completely wrong for this slipper," he said.

"You may not say so," said Gudrun rudely. She sat down on a chair, kicked off her shoe, and put her plump pink foot on the velvet cushion. Of

course, the slipper didn't fit, though she tried hard to squeeze her foot into it.

"You'll crack it!" said the messenger. "Next one, please."

Griselda took her sister's place, but her foot was far too long.

The messenger looked at his list carefully.

"It says here that there is another girl in the household."

"Oh no, that's a mistake," said Griselda. "She is only the kitchen maid."

"No!" Cinderella's father had come into the room. "She is not the kitchen maid, she is my own dear daughter. She has asked to be allowed to try on the slipper."

Cinderella crept into the room behind her father. Her face was dirty because she had just been sweeping the chimney, and her old dress hung in rags. 'Surely this young maid could not possibly be the beautiful stranger,' thought the messenger. But the list said three daughters, and this was the third.

And, of course, the slipper fitted perfectly. The messenger jumped up with excitement and sent a servant to the palace with the good news.

Very soon afterwards, the Prince arrived. He knew his lovely dancing partner immediately, in spite of her ragged clothes and dirty face.

"I thought I would never see you again," he said, taking Cinderella into his arms. "And now that I've found you, will you marry me, my beautiful princess?"

Of course, Cinderella said she would. And because she was as kind as she was beautiful, she asked both her stepsisters and her stepmother to the wedding, which was the happiest and the most magnificent event ever seen in that land.

THE SNOW QUEEN

THIS is a story about a little boy called Kay and his friend, Gerda. But the tale really begins with a magician with a magic mirror. This mirror would shrink everything that was good and beautiful into almost nothing, while ugly and unpleasant things were increased in size, so that they looked even worse than they did before. Now one day his assistants took the mirror and flew with it into the sky. Somehow they let it slip from their hands, and it fell down to earth and shattered into a thousand pieces. Several of these little pieces of mirror flew straight into people's eyes, making everything they looked at seem twisted. But the worst thing of all was when a little splinter of the mirror flew into someone's heart. Immediately, the heart would become as cold and hard as ice.

This is what happened to the little boy, Kay, as you shall hear. Kay and Gerda lived next door to one another. In the summer they would play together, or sit on their two little stools in the bright sunshine, laughing and chatting among the roses that grew everywhere. In the winter, when it was too cold to go outside, they would sit at the window and smile at each other through the frosted glass where they had melted a little hole.

One evening, when Kay was looking out of the window, he saw a huge snowflake drift down to a snow-filled flowerpot. The flake grew larger and larger until at last it took on the shape of a beautiful lady dressed in white. Her ice-cold eyes gleamed like stars, and her gown glittered with frost. She was very beautiful. She beckoned to Kay, but he backed away, frightened.

By the time spring came round again, Kay had forgotten all about the Snow Queen. He played with Gerda in the springtime and in the warm summer days that followed. They could not have been happier. Then, one day, as they were both sitting under the shade of a tree, Kay suddenly cried out.

"There's something in my eye! And oh, I have such a pain round my heart."

He did not know it, but two splinters from the Magic Mirror had flown into his eye and pierced his heart.

"Oh, what's the matter?" cried Gerda. "You look so pale and strange. Are you hurt?"

Kay looked at his friend with ice-cold eyes. "Oh don't fuss," he snapped. "I'm all right. It's just you that looks terribly ugly."

Poor Gerda! Kay had never spoken to her like this before. And as the summer wore on, the Magic Mirror's evil power took hold of him, Kay became a different boy. Gone was the kind and caring friend Gerda had

known. Kay laughed at people and mimicked them, not caring if he upset them or not. And most of all, he laughed at Gerda.

When winter arrived, Kay longed to go out into the snow. He dressed up warmly, took his sledge, and called out to Gerda, "I'm off to the village square. The other boys are going sledging."

"Can I come too?"

"No, of course you can't. You're only a silly, little girl."

When Kay arrived in the square, he found the other boys tying their sledges to the farmer's carts and gliding along in the snow behind them.

'What fun!' thought Kay. When a tall, white-cloaked figure drew up in a big, white sledge, Kay tied his little sledge to the big one. Off they went through the snowy streets of the town!

Very soon, they had passed through the city gates, and sped onwards towards the forest. The snow began to fall very thickly, and the star-shaped snowflakes grew bigger and bigger. At first Kay was excited, but very soon he wanted to go home. With frozen fingers, he tried to unhitch his little sledge from the big one, but he could not manage it. Very frightened, he cried out.

The big sledge stopped, and the white-clad figure turned around to look at him.

It was the Snow Queen, the beautiful lady he had seen the winter before!

"Poor little boy," she said to him. "Come up beside me and I'll wrap you in my fur-rug to keep you warm."

Kay climbed up, and the Snow Queen put her arm around him. He began to feel sleepy.

'I must go back to Grandmother,' he thought. But the Snow Queen gave him an ice-cold kiss; and the little boy's heart, already cold with the splinter from the Magic Mirror, felt icier still. But soon he began to get used to the cold. He felt better, and all thoughts of home, Grandmother, and his friend, Gerda faded. He saw only the beautiful Snow Queen, with her white, fur-lined cloak, and the glittering snowflakes clinging to her dress.

And so they glided onwards through the dark night, through the forests where wolves howled, and across snow-spangled plains.

Very soon, Kay drifted off to sleep, with the Snow Queen's arms around him.

Back at home, Gerda was trying to find out what had happened to Kay. The boys told her he had driven off at the back of a big, white sledge, but no one knew the rider. And though she and Kay's grandmother searched for him all through the winter, they did not find him.

Everyone now thought that Kay was dead, but Gerda did not believe it. When spring came around once again, she set off to look for him.

First she went to the river. Had it carried Kay off downstream? She stepped into a little boat, which gently floated away, carrying Gerda with it. She drifted downstream, past green fields where sheep grazed, until at last she caught sight of a little cottage with a garden full of roses. Gerda's eyes filled with tears, for she could not help remembering the roses that grew back at home in the garden where she and Kay used to play on summer evenings.

'Perhaps someone is at home,' thought Gerda. 'I am so hungry.' She called out, and immediately the cottage door opened. An old lady, bent with age, and carrying a stick came out. She was wearing a beautiful, large hat with flowers on it. She reached out over the river with her stick and pulled Gerda to the bank.

"What are you doing here, little girl?" the old lady asked, and Gerda told her all about her quest to find Kay. "Has he passed this way?" she asked, and the old lady shook her head.

"Not yet," she said, "but why not come in and rest before you continue

[61]

your journey? You can see how pretty it is here, and my little cottage is very comfortable."

"It's lovely," said Gerda. "It reminds me so much of the garden at home – and of Kay."

The old lady took Gerda by the hand and they went inside. It was a beautiful cottage. The sunlight streamed through the windows onto a big bowl of cherries on the table.

"Help yourself," said the old lady. Gerda sat down, and the old lady combed the little girl's hair.

"I have always longed for a child like this," the old lady sighed to herself. "I would like her to live with me." The old lady was a witch, and as she combed Gerda's hair, she wove a spell to make her forget all about her journey to find Kay. However, she knew that if Gerda saw the roses in the garden again, she would remember everything.

The witch went out into the garden and waved her stick over the rose bushes. They immediately sank down under the soil, and no one could tell that they had ever grown there. In their place, the witch put every other type of beautiful flower.

For a while, Gerda played happily in the garden. When she was tired, the old lady tucked her into a little bed, with silk sheets. Gerda slept soundly till morning, with not a thought of Kay in her mind at all.

The next day she was again out in the garden. Every now and again, she stopped and frowned. There was something not quite right – something missing . . .

And then Gerda caught sight of the old lady's hat.

It had roses on it.

"I know," she cried. "There were roses – but where have they gone?" Gerda was very sad that the roses had disappeared, and she began to cry. Her tears fell on a spot where a rose bush had grown. The little bush sprang up and flowered in front of her eyes.

Immediately she remembered everything. She could not stay with the old woman a minute longer. She must continue looking for Kay.

"Have you seen him?" she asked the rose-bush, but it told her that deep down in the earth there was no sign of her little friend.

"He is not dead then," she said, and she ran around the garden, asking each flower if they knew anything about what had happened to Kay. But though each flower told her a magical story, not one could tell her where Kay could be found.

'I must go now,' thought Gerda. 'Before the old lady can keep me a minute longer.' And she ran quickly out of the garden and away from the cottage. She walked on for a long time. She noticed that the weather was turning colder and colder, and that snow was beginning to fall. Suddenly she caught sight of a Raven sitting on the bare branch of a tree.

"Have you seen my friend, Kay?" she asked. "Has a little boy passed this way?"

"It is possible that I have seen him," replied the Raven. "But I have bad news for you. I think he has left you for a Princess."

"A Princess!"

"This Princess," said the Raven, "is well-known for her cleverness and wit. Since she needed someone who was equally clever to talk with her, young men from all over the kingdom came to the Palace. Though they seemed lively and handsome enough, not one of them was as clever as the Princess – until one day a boy arrived at the Palace. He had long, blond hair, but wore the clothes of a peasant."

"That sounds just like Kay!" cried Gerda, in excitement.

"Anyway," went on the Raven, "this boy came to the Princess. He was so handsome, clever and lively that the Princess fell for him at once. And he liked her, too. Believe me, this is all true, for I have a Raven friend within the Palace who has told me all about it."

"Oh, this is certainly Kay!" cried Gerda. "You must let me into the Palace to see him. Once he knows I am here, he will come immediately."

"I will certainly take you there," said the Raven. "And my friend from the Palace will lead you to your friend by a back staircase, for no one will let you in at the main entrance, because you look so shabby."

Gerda followed behind the Raven who flapped and fluttered his way to the Palace and through the grounds. His Raven friend had left a back door open for them, and in they went.

'Oh, how I long to see him at last!' thought Gerda. 'How pleased he will be that I've come so far to find him. How he will long to be home with me once again, and see the rose-trees, and his dear grandmother!'

They went along a corridor and up a grand staircase. Gerda gasped with wonder at all the grand rooms they passed through. At last they came to the Princess's own room, and Gerda saw a young man standing at the window with the Princess.

"Kay!" she cried, and ran forward. The young man turned, and it was not Kay at all! Gerda burst into disappointed tears because she was so unhappy. She told the Princess all that had happened to her, and how the Raven had helped her to find Kay.

"But we were wrong," she sobbed. "He isn't here at all." The Princess smiled kindly at her.

"Stay here in the Palace for the night and rest," she said. "In the morning we will give you a carriage and fresh clothes. You will feel so much better then."

Gerda slept soundly that night, and her dreams were pleasant ones. In the morning, she found a dress of silk, a cloak of velvet laid out for her, and a little, white fur muff to keep her hands warm. The Princess accompanied her to the Palace entrance and a golden coach drew up for her.

"Good luck with your quest," said the Princess, as the coach drove off.

"Thank you for everything," said Gerda. "And thank you, too, dear Raven, for all your kindness."

"I will fly behind the coach for the first part of your journey," he said, and he fluttered along beside the coach for many miles.

The coach drove through a dark forest, but alas, it was seen by a band of robbers who saw it gleaming through the trees. They pushed the coachmen to the ground and seized hold of Gerda.

"Shall I kill her?" said one of the robbers. But her little daughter, who had come with her on the raid, clutched hold of her arm.

"No, Mother," she said. "I want a playmate. Let this little girl stay with me to be my friend."

And because the little robber girl was so spoilt, her mother spared Gerda's life and let the two girls travel back to the robber camp in the golden coach. As they went along, Gerda told the robber girl all about her search for Kay and the adventures she had along the way.

"Well, now the adventures are over," said the robber girl. "I want you to stay with me and be my friend. I will show you my pets. You'll see what a wonderful time we'll have together."

But when Gerda arrived at the robber camp, she found that the robber girl's pets were a poor old reindeer who was chained to the wall all day, and a hundred pigeons, which she kept imprisoned in one room. The robber girl teased them terribly and waved a dagger at the reindeer's throat.

"I have my dagger with me always," she boasted. "I even sleep with it!" And she pulled Gerda down on a straw mattress and put one arm around her neck. The other held the dagger. There was no way Gerda could escape.

It was a terrible night and Gerda slept very badly. But as she lay awake during the long hours, she heard a pigeon cooing at her.

"We have seen your Kay," it said. "He passed through our forest with the Snow Queen."

"The Snow Queen!" cried Gerda. "Where will I find her? Where does she live?"

"Why not ask the Reindeer over there? He'll know."

The Reindeer told Gerda that the Snow Queen was probably in Lapland, where she stayed for the summer. In winter she travelled off to an island near the North Pole.

Gerda cried out, when she heard how far away Kay had been taken, and the robber girl woke up.

"Keep quiet, or I'll stab you with my dagger," she threatened.

In the morning, though, the robber girl was in a better mood. She had grown fond of Gerda and did not like to see her so sad.

"I will help you find Kay," she said. "My reindeer will take you to Lapland, to the castle of the Snow Queen."

The Reindeer's eyes shone at the thought of his own freedom, and Gerda could scarcely believe that the robber girl was letting her go.

"You will need warm clothes," said the robber girl. "Take my mother's gloves. They are far too big for you, but they will cover your arms."

After giving Gerda food and drink for the journey, the robber girl waved goodbye. Gerda saw her standing by the door, with two huge guard dogs at her side, and her dagger gleaming in the sunlight.

For a time, Aladdin and his mother lived very well. Whenever they needed more food, they would call the Genie.

One day, the Emperor's daughter passed by in her golden carriage. Everyone was told to keep off the streets so that the Princess could drive by in comfort. But Aladdin hid himself so that he could catch a glimpse of her.

Minutes later he came running in, his eyes shining.

"Mother! I have seen the Princess!" he cried. "She is the most beautiful girl in the world and I want to marry her."

"What nonsense!" snapped his mother. "How can you, a commoner, hope to marry a Princess?"

"Listen!" said Aladdin in excitement. "We have the jewel-fruits from the garden. Take those to the Emperor as a gift from me, Mother. He will not be able to resist them."

The next morning, Aladdin's mother went to the royal palace. The Grand Vizier led her to the Emperor. He was completely dazzled by the jewels.

"Your son must be a very rich man," he said. "He is quite worthy to be the husband of my daughter, the Princess."

But the Grand Vizier had plans for his own son to marry the Emperor's daughter.

"You do not know the fellow," he told the Emperor. "Tell this woman you will need three months to consider things."

In the three months that Aladdin's mother was waiting for her second visit, the Grand Vizier managed to persuade the Emperor that his own son would make the best husband for the Princess.

One day when Aladdin's mother was in the market-place, she saw great preparations being made for a grand wedding.

"Who is to be married?" she asked someone.

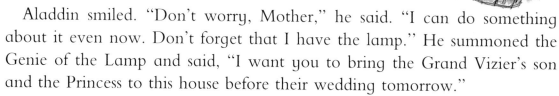

"Why, the Princess – have you not heard? She is marrying the Grand Vizier's son."

Aladdin's mother hurried home and told Aladdin all about it.

Aladdin smiled. "Don't worry, Mother," he said. "I can do something about it even now. Don't forget that I have the lamp." He summoned the Genie of the Lamp and said, "I want you to bring the Grand Vizier's son and the Princess to this house before their wedding tomorrow."

"It shall be done, young master," said the Genie. Before Aladdin could tidy himself up for the Princess, the young couple stood before him, dazed and afraid.

Aladdin seized hold of the Grand Vizier's son and shut him in a cupboard. Then he took the Princess by the hand.

"I want to marry you," he said simply. "Your father the Emperor cheated me. He promised to wait three months before giving his answer to my claim for your hand. But he didn't wait and chose the Grand Vizier's son instead."

The Princess gazed at the young man standing before her. How much more handsome he was than her bridegroom!

"I will send you back to the Palace by magic," Aladdin went on. "Tell no one what has happened. But say instead that you no longer wish to marry the Grand Vizier's son."

The Princess found this was an easy promise to make, for she had already fallen in love with this astonishing young man. The Genie took the Princess back to the palace and Aladdin released the Grand Vizier's son from the cupboard. The young bridegroom was so frightened by what had happened that he asked the Emperor to cancel the wedding immediately. He wanted nothing more to do with such powerful magic.

At the end of the three months, Aladdin's mother went again to the

Emperor with Aladdin's request to marry the Princess. "I will give my word that your son will marry my daughter," said the Emperor. "But only if you bring me a hundred silver trays laden with jewels." The Emperor had no wish for the Princess to marry a complete stranger and thought that it would be impossible for her to carry out such a task. He was mistaken. Within an hour, a hundred servants appeared, each bearing a silver tray laden with precious gems.

"How can I say no now?" exclaimed the Emperor. He immediately sent for the young man who had sent such a generous gift. Aladdin soon appeared dressed in all his finery, for the Genie had given him all the rich clothes and jewels he needed to present himself at the palace. As soon as he saw Aladdin, all of the Emperor's doubts vanished. Here was a son-in-law to be proud of! He immediately gave his consent.

"Before we are married," promised Aladdin, "I will build the Princess a splendid palace."

And he did so within a week. The Emperor could scarcely believe the magnificent building that grew before his very eyes. It was built of marble and decorated with gold. Silver fountains played in the courtyards, and in the stables fifty fine Arab horses stamped and shook their fine leather bridles.

And so Aladdin married his Princess. He was popular with all of the Emperor's subjects, for he was generous and kind. He and the Princess were blissfully happy together – until a few months later when something terrible happened.

Aladdin had by now long forgotten the wicked magician. However, the magician had not forgotten Aladdin nor the magic lamp which was the cause of Aladdin's good fortune. One day when Aladdin was out hunting, the magician came to the palace gates, disguised as an old lamp-seller. He shouted, "New lamps for old! New lamps for old!"

The Princess leaned out the window.

"What lovely, new, shiny lamps!" she exclaimed. She remembered that Aladdin had a dirty old lamp, and she ordered a servant to fetch it for her.

"Aladdin will be so pleased that I've bought him a new lamp, and replaced that horrible old one," she said, very pleased with herself.

Of course, this was exactly what the magician wanted! He grabbed the old lamp and tucked it under his cloak. As soon as he was out of sight of the palace, he rubbed it. Immediately the Genie appeared. He had a new master now.

"Take Aladdin's palace back to my homeland," he ordered the Genie. Before the poor Princess knew what had happened to her, she found herself flying through the air in her palace of marble.

Poor Aladdin! When he returned home, he found just an empty space where his palace had stood. The Grand Vizier ordered Aladdin to be brought to his master to explain himself.

"Where is my daughter?" thundered the Emperor. "What has happened to the palace?"

"I have always suspected that this young man is a magician," the Grand Vizier whispered in the Emperor's ear. He had never forgiven Aladdin for displacing his son.

The Emperor did not know what to do. He was fond of his son-in-law, and he knew the people loved him. If he ordered Aladdin to be executed, there would be a riot, and it would not bring his daughter back to him.

"I will give you forty days to find my daughter," the Emperor said at last. "If you have no news of her by the end of that time, then you will be severely punished."

Aladdin was glad that he would not be killed, but he did not know where to begin looking for the Princess. He left the Emperor's palace, wishing with all of his heart that he still had his magic lamp. Then suddenly he remembered that, though he didn't have the lamp, he did have the ring the magician had first given to him. Trembling with excitement, he rubbed it. Sure enough, the Genie appeared.

"I am the Genie of the Ring," he said. "What does my master wish me to do?"

"Take me to my Palace," said Aladdin. "Take me to my Princess."

Immediately he found himself standing outside his very own palace, but it was in the middle of a strange land. He called out, and the Princess leaned out of a window.

"Oh, you have come at last, my love," she said, and she ran down to let him in.

"Where is the lamp?" asked Aladdin after he had embraced his wife. "If we are to get out of this place, I must have it."

"The magician keeps it with him always," said the Princess. "I don't know how I can take it from him."

Aladdin pulled a bottle from his pocket. "Listen to me," he said. "When the magician sits with you to eat, pour some of this into his wine. He will suspect nothing, for he does not know that I am here."

The Princess did exactly as Aladdin had told her. Secretly, she shook some drops of poison from the bottle into his wine glass. Minutes later, the wicked magician raised his glass to her. "To my beautiful princess," he said mockingly. "May we live together for many happy years, hidden from that troublesome husband of yours." He tipped back the glass, drank deeply, and immediately fell lifeless at her feet.

The Princess pulled the lamp from under his robes and ran to find Aladdin.

"Here it is!" she cried breathlessly. "Now we can go home!"

The next morning when the Emperor awoke, he looked out from his window. He could barely believe his eyes.

There stood Aladdin's palace, back in its rightful place. And there in the courtyard were Aladdin and his precious daughter.

"There is magic in all this – the Grand Vizier is right! But now that I have my daughter back and the best son-in-law I could wish for, what does it matter?" Years later when the old Emperor died, Aladdin became Emperor in his place. And a very wise and generous ruler he was too.

THE LITTLE MATCH GIRL

IT was terribly cold. The snow fell, covering the roads and roofs of the big city. It was New Year's Eve, the very last night of the year. Inside the big houses, people were eating, drinking and dancing, while under glittering Christmas trees, all covered with candles, the children played.

Outside in the snowy street, a little girl was hurrying along. She had a thin, ragged cloak and bare, frozen feet. When she had left home that morning, she had worn a pair of slippers. They were too big for her and had fallen off and been lost during the day. She carried with her a small bundle of matches, for she was a Match Girl who sold them for a living. That day she had been very unlucky. She had not sold one match or earned any money at all. People had been too busy hurrying home in the snow to the warmth and comfort of their homes, to spare a thought for the little, frozen, starving girl.

She was a pretty child with long, golden hair. Her little body was painfully thin; and her cheeks, usually pale and pinched, were now red with the cold. As she hurried along, she saw through every window the lights of candles and lamps and the warm glow from countless stoves. In some windows she saw people laughing and talking. In others she saw tables all set with more food than she had eaten in her entire life. The Little Match Girl's mouth watered as she imagined the smell of the roast meat, the warm, thick soup and the spicy puddings.

Very soon, the Little Match Girl's footsteps grew slower and slower until at last she stopped altogether and huddled in a corner between two houses. It was not just the cold that made her stop here. She knew she would be in trouble when she reached the attic that was home. For when her father knew that she had sold no matches, he would beat her.

'The matches!' she thought. 'Perhaps the light from their flames will warm me.' So the Little Match Girl lit one match and held her hands over the warm glow. She sighed happily as the match began to warm her hands. The bright, flickering light made it seem that she was no longer crouched in her dark, cold corner. Instead, she was sitting beside a large stove that glowed with warmth and comfort.

"How wonderful it feels!" she said, and she stretched out her poor, frozen feet to warm them. But before she could do so, the flame died away, and the stove vanished. Once more she found herself on the pavement, leaning against the cold stone of the house.

'Perhaps if I light another match, I will see the stove again,' she thought. When she did so, she found she could see right through the walls of the house into the room behind it. There was a long table there, covered with a white cloth with plate after plate of mouth-watering food. There was a huge joint of roast turkey, and it seemed to the Little Match Girl that she was near enough to carve herself a thick slice of it. But even as she reached out to take a knife, the match burnt down and the flame died. Instead of the festive room, the Little Match Girl was once again outside in the snowy street, crouched against the hard, stone wall.

Her fingers were so frozen that she could scarcely move them to light the third match, but at last she managed it. How glad she was that she did so. Now she was sitting under a beautiful Christmas tree that was ablaze with a hundred candles. Glass balls and little wooden angels hung from its branches. The Little Match Girl had never seen anything so wonderful in her life. At home there was only a single candle to light the little, bare attic room. The Little Match Girl stared and stared. She did not notice the match go out. The tree did not fade away as everything had done before. The lights on the branches flared higher and higher, and one fell down from the top of the tree. "It looks exactly like a falling star," said the Little Match Girl. "My grandmother always said that a falling star means that someone has died." Her eyes filled with tears as she remembered her grandmother. She had been the only person who had ever loved her, and now she was dead.

The Christmas Tree faded and the Little Match Girl lit a fourth match. She gave a cry, for there in front of her was the one person she thought she would never see again.

"Grandmother!" she cried. "You have come back to me! Oh, I must quickly light the other matches or else you will fade away."

Fumbling in her bundle with her numb, cold fingers, the Little Match Girl lit all of the remaining matches. The light from them shone into her cold corner and stretched out into the snowy, cold streets of the city. The

Little Match Girl shielded her eyes from the brilliant light and looked up. Her grandmother still stood there and she seemed to grow taller and taller. Her face shone with beauty and kindness. She stooped down and took the Little Match Girl's cold hands in her own. Then she gathered her up in her arms and flew with her over the city, just as the bells from all the churches rang in the New Year.

They flew higher and higher until the coldness of this world gave way to the brilliance of Paradise.

The next morning, the people from the house where the Little Match Girl had found shelter looked out their door.

"Oh dear, how sad!" they cried. "There's a little girl out here. She must have frozen to death."

For the Little Match Girl lay there. She did not look dead, for her cheeks were glowing and there was a happy smile on her face. But she had died with the Old Year at midnight. Around her lay a pile of spent matches.

"Oh look, she tried to warm herself to keep alive," said the lady of the house. "Poor little thing. And so beautiful, too!"

Not one of them knew of the wonderful things the Little Match Girl had seen in the last hours of her life. And they did not know that now, up in Heaven, she was celebrating the best New Year ever with her beloved grandmother.

THE UGLY DUCKLING

BY the side of a large lake, a mother duck was hatching her eggs. One, two, three, four, five little ducklings hopped out of the broken shells; but the biggest egg of all still lay in the nest, unbroken.

"It looks like a turkey's egg to me," said Father Duck, who had come to see his new family.

"Oh no," said Mother Duck. "It will hatch into a big, handsome, strong duckling. You'll see!"

At that moment there was a loud 'crack' and the egg burst open. Both Mother Duck and Father Duck stared. A skinny creature with a long neck and gangly legs scrambled out. It was not like a duckling at all.

"I told you, it is a turkey!" quacked Father Duck in disgust, and he flew off angrily.

Mother Duck gathered her new duckling under her wings.

"I don't care what that good-for-nothing husband of mine says about you," she said. "I think you are beautiful."

That morning, Mother Duck pushed her brood into the waters of the lake. They all began to swim at once, even the big, ugly one.

"There! I said you weren't a turkey!" said Mother Duck, swimming proudly with her little family across the lake to the other side. When they had all scrambled onto dry land again, Mother Duck said, "Now, Ducklings, the world is a very large place, and I am going to show you something of it. Over there is a farmyard. I will begin by taking you to see the Most Important Duck of all."

The five little ducklings and the one big ugly one all quacked with excitement. What fun it would be to meet some other ducks! But when they reached the farmyard, all the chickens and ducks crowded around them.

"So this is your new family," said the Most Important Duck of all. "Well, five of them are very pretty, I'll say that. But that big, clumsy one – what sort of a duck is that supposed to be?"

And as the Very Important Duck spoke, she prodded the poor Ugly Duckling with her long bill.

"Quack, quack, cluck, cluck," went all the chickens and ducks. They pecked and flapped at the Ugly Duckling, making him run all around the farmyard and into a patch of nettles where he could not be seen.

Mother Duck came to look for him. "Never mind," she said. "I love you, even if the others are unkind. Take no notice of them."

The Ugly Duckling's life was made miserable by the other birds and animals on the farm. Wherever he went, he was kicked and pecked and chased. Even his five little brothers and sisters joined in. At last he could bear it no longer.

"I am so ugly that no one can stand me," he sobbed to himself. "Well, then, I will go right away and live alone and look after myself."

So the very next time the hens chased him around the yard, he ran out through a hole in the hedge and said goodbye to the farmyard for ever.

The Ugly Duckling ran and fluttered on for miles, until at last he came to a moor where the wild ducks lived. He was now so tired that he tucked his head under his wing and fell fast asleep.

The next morning, the wild ducks flew across to him.

"Who are you?" asked one of them. "Where have you come from?"

"You are very ugly," said another, and the poor Ugly Duckling felt worse than ever.

"I am told so," he said, humbly. "But will you let me stay with you, ugly or not?"

The wild ducks said that he could live with them if he wished. The Duckling stayed with them for several days, swimming peacefully in the lake that lay in the middle of the moor.

One morning, the ducks were joined by a flock of geese.

"Aren't you ugly?" hissed the geese. But before the Duckling could reply, there was a loud 'Bang' and the geese flew off, terrified.

'What is happening?' thought the Duckling, and he tried to hide himself among the reeds.

"Bang! Bang! Bang!" There were more horrible noises. The Duckling did not know that the sounds were guns and that men were out on the moor hunting for geese and ducks. He shut his eyes and tried to hide his head under his wing to shut out the sound, but it was no good. The noises went on for hours and hours. When he eventually opened his eyes, he saw a large dog staring at him, with his tongue hanging out of his mouth. How big and fierce he looked! The Ugly Duckling trembled with fright. Then, just as he thought the dog would seize hold of him, the animal turned around and splashed away through the reeds.

"I am even too ugly for the dog to eat me!" said the Ugly Duckling sadly. "But never mind. At least I am alive."

The shooting went on for the rest of the day. At last, as the sun was setting, it stopped. The Ugly Duckling stayed in the reeds for some time, too frightened to move. There was no sign of the ducks or the geese. 'Perhaps they have flown away, or perhaps they have been shot,' he thought. At last the young Duckling poked his head out of the reeds and looked all around him. The men and the dogs had gone and the moor was quiet at last.

"I must move on. It is not safe here," said the Ugly Duckling. He shook his feathers and set out across the moor. He ran and he fluttered until at last he came to a ramshackle little cottage on the edge of the moor. A strong wind had risen, and the Ugly Duckling was nearly blown away. But suddenly, the wind blew the door of the cottage open, just a little, and the Duckling was able to creep into the cottage for shelter.

Now in the cottage there lived an old woman with her tom-cat and her hen. She loved both of them, for the tom-cat would warm her lap and purr and the hen would lay her a nice brown egg each day. She spotted the Ugly Duckling at once; but because her eyesight was not good, she thought he was a big, fat duck. "How lovely!" she exclaimed. "Now I shall have duck's eggs as well as hen's eggs."

For three weeks the old lady looked for duck's eggs, but of course the poor Duckling could not produce any. Now the Cat and the Hen were the most important animals in the cottage and thought they knew everything. When the Duckling timidly gave his opinion on things, the Hen asked him, "Can you lay eggs?"

"No," said the Ugly Duckling.

"Well, then, hold your tongue!"

And the Cat said, "Can you arch your back? Can you purr?"

"No," said the Ugly Duckling.

"Then you should have no opinion at all."

The Duckling was not at all happy in the cottage. He sat in a corner and began to long for the fresh air again.

"How I wish I was swimming in the sunshine," he told the Hen. "How I wish I could dive down and catch insects in the mud at the bottom of the lake."

The Hen thought this was a very strange idea and said so. The cat joined in.

"You are not only ugly, but stupid too. Do you ever see our wise old woman diving for insects? Do you ever see Hen or me swimming on the lake?"

"No," said the Duckling.

"Well, as we three are the cleverest in the world, then you must be stupid for wanting these things. Here you are, nice and snug in a warm room. You don't lay eggs and you don't purr. You are completely useless."

The Cat and the Hen turned their backs on the Duckling and went to sleep by the fire.

"I know when I'm not wanted," said the Duckling to himself. "Ah well, I am better on my own. I will go off and find a nice patch of water to swim on."

That night, he squeezed through a crack under the door and set off on his travels again. He soon came to a lake and splashed happily into it, diving to the bottom to catch insects. He was beginning to feel rather lonely, though. All the other animals and birds ignored him because he was different and ugly. By now, winter was well on its way. The leaves were turning gold, and the nights were growing colder.

Late one afternoon when the sun was setting, the Ugly Duckling suddenly saw something strange and wonderful. A flock of large birds rose from the reeds and flew off over his head. They were dazzling white, and they uttered strange, wild cries that made the Ugly Duckling feel sad and happy at the same time. Then they flew up, higher and higher, until their feathers glowed pink and gold in the sunset.

The Ugly Duckling craned his neck and watched them until they disappeared. 'How beautiful they were,' he thought. 'How graceful and how free!' All that night, the next day, and for many days to come, the Duckling thought and dreamed about the birds.

'I am far too ugly to be their friend,' he thought. 'But if I could just swim along beside them, I would be happy enough.'

Winter was now here. The days and nights grew colder still, and frost glistened on the trees. The lake began to freeze over. At first the Ugly Duckling swam round and round in the bit of water that was left, but each night the lake froze a little more. The Duckling's hole grew smaller and smaller, until one morning he found he was frozen solid in the ice.

Poor Ugly Duckling! He nearly died of the cold. But later that morning, a farmer passed by the lake and saw him lying frozen in the water. He took his wooden shoe, broke the ice, and tucked the nearly dead Duckling in his coat. He would take him home for his children. They had always wanted a pet. The farmer gave the Duckling to his wife and she put him beside the fire. Very gradually, the Ugly Duckling unfroze.

"Come here, children!" called the farmer's wife. "Just look at what your father has brought home to you!"

The children shrieked with delight. They all ran towards the Duckling who was recovering in front of the fire. He was terrified. He flapped and fluttered around the room and jumped into a pail of milk. It fell on its side and there was milk everywhere. Then he ran across the table, upsetting the dishes and the food.

"Catch that Duckling!" cried the farmer's wife. All the children shouted and giggled and ran after the frightened bird.

"Take that!" cried the farmer's wife, and she hit the Ugly Duckling with a ladle. She would have hit him again; but when the Duckling saw that the door was open, he fled outside and away across the farmyard into the fields beyond.

It was a terribly hard winter. The Duckling spent some time by the frozen lake, and he only just managed to keep alive. He grew hungrier and hungrier and he thought he would die. Then one day, he noticed that the sun was shining more warmly and the birds were singing more cheerfully. Little flowers and green leaves began to grow around him, and the waters of the lake unfroze. Spring had arrived!

The Ugly Duckling decided to move on once more. On the other side of the lake he found a river and started to swim down it. He felt the warmth of the sun on his feathers, and he stretched out his wings. How big they were! He folded them over his back and swam on. Suddenly, as he swam round a bend in the river, he saw three beautiful, white birds ahead of him. Why, they were the same birds he had seen and dreamed about a few months ago! He trembled with wonder and fear. They were so large and powerful. They were gliding silently down the river, their necks curved gracefully and their feathers gleaming in the sun.

"Oh, I must speak to them!" cried the Ugly Duckling. "I don't mind if they laugh at me and call me ugly. I don't even mind if they kill me. I would rather be killed by such beautiful birds than be pecked to death by chickens!"

He swam quickly towards them. They heard his splash in the water and turned round. The poor Ugly Duckling was too modest to look the birds in the eye. He bent his long neck and said to them, "I had to speak to you. I had to tell you how wonderful you look gliding on the river. You can kill me if you like – I don't care. But at least I have spoken to you."

"Why are you so shy?" asked one of the birds gently. "Why do you find us so wonderful?"

"Because you are beautiful, white, graceful birds, and I am only an Ugly Duckling."

"An Ugly Duckling? Just look at your reflection in the water," said the second. "Don't you see?"

And the Ugly Duckling opened his eyes and stared. Gone was his ugly,

clumsy shape. Below him, reflected in the water, was a beautiful white bird!

"You are a Swan," explained the third. "We are all Swans. Didn't you know?"

"No, I didn't," sighed the young Swan happily. "Everyone told me I was ugly, and I thought I always would be. I had no idea I would become a Swan."

The three Swans stroked him with their beaks. "Welcome to our river," they said. "You must join us and live with us for ever."

The young Swan had found a home and friends at last!

Soon the Swans came to a large house by the side of the river. Several children were playing on the bank.

"Look! Look!" cried one. "The swans have returned!"

"And there's a new one among them," said another.

"And he is the most beautiful of all," exclaimed the third. The young Swan felt his heart burst with happiness.